COWBOY FOR CHRISTMAS

Rescued by the Cowboy at Christmas - Book 3
By J. A. Somers

Cowboy for Christmas

Rescued by the Cowboy at Christmas, Volume 3

J. A. Somers

Published by J. A. Somers, 2023.

COWBOY FOR CHRISTMAS

First edition. August 8, 2023.

Copyright © 2023 J. A. Somers.

ISBN: 979-8223174592

Written by J. A. Somers.

Table of Contents

COWBOY FOR CHRISTMAS

Cameron Charming is going to put Christmas on hold this year and focus on his work instead. He'd lost his family during the holidays a while back. His plans to remain grumpy over the Christmas season are thwarted when he meets a charming red-headed beauty with a fiery personality.

Seriously? Cat cannot believe her luck. She's stuck outside in the small town of Mistletoe over the holidays. The blogger-turned-author has a tight deadline to meet but she can't get into her cozy cabin to finish her manuscript. And to top it off, a terrible storm is brewing. Then...a handsome cowboy shows up.

Can two people, determined to remain single, get caught up in the spirit of the Christmas season?

Chapter 1

Oh no! This can't be happening!

Catherine "Cat" Smith could not believe her luck. She blew out a puff of air in the dark wintery night sky as she sighed heavily. The key was stuck in the lock of her cabin's front door.

Her teeth clattered as she fought to keep warm.

What was she going to do now?

She could not believe this was happening. She had just gotten back to her hometown of Mistletoe after signing her first book deal. Her publisher had given her an advance and she decided the perfect writing spot to finish her manuscript would be in this rented cabin for a month—away from distraction. She lived in New York with her roommates and there was no way she could get the book done in time for the deadline if she stayed there with all the noise.

The money from the advance was generous and it not only paid for the cabin for the month of December but it was enough to cover the fees for her grandfather's care at the retirement home in New York for the next twelve months. She'd been taking care of him with the money she'd been making from her blog ever since his stroke and since her grandmother had passed.

When her folks passed when she was in her teens, her grandfather had raised her. She would do anything for him. She was glad she was in a position to be there for him and to help him too. In fact, he always encouraged her to follow her dream of writing for a living.

Luckily, being a content creator, she could work from anywhere as long as she had a laptop computer, Wi-Fi connection and electricity.

Right now, she could use some Wi-Fi *and* some electricity to keep her warm.

She tried the lock again. The key still wouldn't work. Her agent had arranged for her cabin retreat and accommodation in Mistletoe. Did he send her the wrong key?

She had to turn in the final draft of her book by Christmas. Her book was due to be released in the new year by February. The publishers were aiming for a Valentine's Day release.

It was ironic that it was a Valentine's Day release since Cat no longer believed in love.

After her ex-fiancé broke off with her after he got what he wanted out of her when she helped him with his college studies, she decided to focus on her own life and help others in the same boat—that's when she created her Singles blog.

How could she have not seen that her ex had been using her? She had pushed her dreams aside while helping him with his—only for him to turn around and dump her for some dancer.

Well, so much for putting her heart on the line. Never again. She was going to focus on her career and taking care of Grandpa. She had no room in her life for anyone else right now.

It was already four weeks till Christmas but that was the best time to be locked away in a cabin, away from holiday carollers and everybody else making a fuss about Christmas. Her grandfather and she stopped celebrating the holiday years ago when her grandmother passed.

She didn't know if she could ever feel the Christmas spirit again since her ex broke off with her over the holidays.

And right now, she knew that Christmas could be hard on the lonely. That's why she decided to distance herself from everyone else right now and focus on her material.

The truth was, she'd hoped to be married by thirty-five. It was her dream to be as happy as her parents were before they went to be with the Lord. But to make herself feel better and protect her heart from any more heartbreak she decided maybe it wasn't for her. She wished she had some sort of sign though. Maybe she should just forget about relationships and help others with theirs. No matter how much she told herself it didn't matter if she never found that special one, there was something inside her, a loneliness that swept over her.

Speaking of sweeping over her. The snow came down heavy like a bale of hay. The chill prickled her skin on her exposed cheeks. She rubbed herself as she shivered outside.

She reached into her bag to pull out her cell phone.

It was dead.

Dead.

Just as she would be soon if she didn't get inside soon, away from the plummeting temperatures.

Her agent was supposed to have everything arranged now including a key that worked. And if she had any power left on her cell phone, she'd call him now and give him a piece of her mind.

She prayed to the Lord to keep her safe out there. She glanced around and it was pitch dark. The streetlights were dimly lit and didn't provide too much light.

Why, oh, why did she tell the Uber driver to leave once she arrived at her destination? She should have told him to wait to see if she could get inside first.

Cat rubbed her arms as she shivered to keep warm. Ice pellets touched her exposed skin on her face.

Right now she wished she was inside her cabin, nice and warm. On nights like this, she was reminded of the times when she *did* celebrate the holidays with her grandparents. She would come in from the bitter winter cold and into the home. Her grandmother would bake the most delicious gingerbread cookies and Cat would love to eat them as soon as they came out of the oven. The aroma of the gingerbread always comforted her. The cookies were always fresh, crispy and warm. Just as warm as she wished she was right now.

Why did that memory sweep into her mind all of a sudden?

She wanted to be comforted. Remembering happier, simpler times.

She then started to walk, her boots crunching on the snow, as she tried to figure out if the back door was open. She didn't think so, of course, but she had no choice but to try.

"Okay, there has to be a way to get inside."

Maybe she should see if there was an opened window she could climb into. She'd already paid for the whole month to rent this cabin. And it wasn't cheap, either.

Just then, she heard a sound coming from the back of the cabin. Was someone hiding back there?

She froze.

Chapter 2

Cameron Charming made his way up the steps to the Children's Center at the Mistletoe Hospital carrying a large red sack full of Christmas presents.

The security guard at the front desk nodded and let him through since he'd been there earlier. He was a regular there.

He'd been volunteering his time there ever since he lost his wife and stepdaughter many years ago in a freak car accident over the holidays. He thought he'd never want to celebrate the holidays again but he'd learned that helping others was a great way to give back and to help in the healing process.

Volunteering his time gave him a chance to reach out to others during their difficult time and to give a helping hand to families in the community.

He walked into the main activity room where the kids were gathered around for storytelling. The place was decorated in twinkling red and green Christmas lights and the fireplace in the corner had lovely red velvet stockings that hung around it. The garland around the electric fireplace reminded him of the one at the main house on the ranch. It gave one a lovely feeling of warmth and joy around the holidays.

In no time, a few of the kids rushed over to him and greeted him.

Seeing their bright smiles when he brought presents for them warmed his heart.

The kids unwrapped their presents with excitement.

Lia, the senior coordinator came by and thanked him again.

"How are you keeping up?" Lia asked him later after he'd finished spending an hour there. She walked with him as he made his way out to the main foyer of the building.

"Good," he said.

"I know it can't be easy for you," she said. "But we really appreciate you coming here every year."

"I'm just glad I could make it," he added.

She smiled.

"Are you coming to the Annual Christmas Barn Hall Dance?" he asked her once they got to the main doors.

"Wouldn't miss it for the world."

Lia was about the same age as his mother. A very nice lady. And like his mother, Lia had tried to play matchmaker for him, telling him it would be nice to move forward. He'd thanked her but told her he was not going to think about relationships for now. Even though it had been four years now to the day. He just wasn't interested in anyone.

"I hope to see you under the magical mistletoe this year," Lia said with a warm smile.

"I don't think that's going to happen, Miss Lia. I think I've passed those days."

"You never know. It's been magical for your brothers." She arched a brow with a grin.

He was happy his brothers had finally found love under the mistletoe during the family's annual Christmas dance. That famous mistletoe always bestowed good luck to those who kissed under it. But this cowboy was sure it wasn't going to happen for him anytime soon. He just didn't feel right moving on. He wanted to hold a candle to his late wife and stepdaughter forever. That's how he felt in his heart right now.

He knew deep down that's not the way the Lord wanted him to live his life. But he had so many issues to work through and he knew it was going to take time. A lot of time.

He placed his cowboy hat back on his head and made his way out the door of the north wing of the hospital, out into the cold winter night.

"Thanks again for coming, Cameron. It's always nice to see you."

"Likewise, Lia."

"And think about what I said. You never know who you'll meet at the dance." She winked.

Oh, boy.

He grinned and shook his head.

That clearly meant Lia had someone in mind for him. Once again.

He didn't want to hurt anyone's feelings though.

But maybe soon they'd see that he was serious when he said he wasn't going to be in another relationship again. Not after losing his family. He just didn't feel right moving on or being happy when they couldn't be here.

Would he ever get over that feeling?

Chapter 3

Cat's heart stopped beating. Her breath halted.

"Who's there?" she called out into the cold dark night as snow blew around her. Too bad the lights in her cabin were off. Of course there was no light inside. She wasn't inside to turn them on. No one was inside. But someone *was* outside her house.

Who was it? A burglar?

She hoped not. They wouldn't find anything inside to take.

But right now she was on deadline with her book and had to turn in her first draft, as per her contract.

"Who's there?" Her voice sounded bolder and stronger. She wasn't afraid. Well, actually, she was, but she wasn't going to let anyone know.

Her handbag was heavy. In fact, her friends always teased her that she could knock someone out with her handbag if she wasn't careful. She held it up to her chest, getting ready to swing it at the intruder.

But it was too late. Something came out at her and she screamed.

It moved quickly and rushed past her.

Oh, thank goodness.

It was a racoon, not an intruder.

Wait a minute. Why was she thankful it was a racoon? It wasn't like he had a key with him or anything to help her get inside her warm cabin.

Well, she assumed it would be warmer inside than outside.

Pushing herself against the heavy winds blowing in her direction, she made her way up the steps leading to the side of the cabin.

Her skin prickled with ice as snow pellets continued to blow around her as if they were attacking her personally.

When she finally climbed toward the back of the cabin, her jaw fell wide open.

Chapter 4

Cameron decided to avoid the town's heavy traffic. He wanted to have a long quiet drive home back to Charming Ranch.

He needed time to think.

He started down on West Street when for some strange reason, he turned down East Street. Why did he do that?

He thought nothing of it at the time. He wanted a long quiet drive so he was going to get one. East Street was more country and had a few cabins spattered about. It was where a lot of recluse people lived. Those who wanted to be closer to nothing but nature and far away from noise in the heaviest part of town.

He couldn't blame them one bit.

Just then a sound came from his truck.

It was his cell phone ringing through the speakers. He had it set up so he didn't have to reach to answer it while driving. His late wife had been the one to insist he have it done. She saved his life.

But he didn't save hers. Or their daughter.

You weren't there, man. You couldn't have saved them. You weren't there.

Well, those words echoing in his mind sure didn't make him feel any better. He should've been there. He should have been there to rescue them, to comfort them, to let them know he was there and everything was going to be all right.

But he didn't.

He couldn't.

And he'd have to live with that guilt for the rest of his life.

The Lord had blessed him with a wonderful family. And look what happened. He was away on business at the time.

He was a broken cowboy.

Too broken to ever love again. He just didn't feel he could ever move forward.

He sighed deeply.

"Hey, what's up?"

"What? No Merry Christmas?" That was the ever-sarcastic voice of his brother Brad.

"No Merry Christmas. You've got that right," Cameron responded.

"Come on, man," his other brother Carter said. They obviously had him on speaker phone.

He was happy for Carter who, after breaking up with his fiancée some Christmases ago, reunited with her and got married. She'd come back one Christmas and explained why she had to break off with him and now they were happily married with a baby on the way.

If there was ever someone who deserved it, it was Carter. And all his brothers, as a matter of fact. They'd all had their share of heartbreak and now they were happily married.

He'd had his chance. He often wondered if that was the only chance at being happily married he'd get.

Did everyone just get one shot at it?

Well, maybe just some people, of which he was probably one of them.

He couldn't save his family. Now there was nothing inside him. Maybe that was his last chance and he blew it.

"Sorry Carter and Brad. I'm just not feeling it right now."

"But Lia said it went well at the Children's Hospital. She said you were in the festive mood. Didn't it go well?"

"It did. You should've seen the look on the kids' faces. It was a pure blessing."

"So what happened? Why are you so down then?" Carter asked.

"Because after I leave, the feeling leaves. It's happened that way ever since..."

He paused and said nothing for a moment. The only sound that could be heard was the sound of the four wheels grinding on the road on this snowy winter night. He wished his family was with him now.

"Man, I'm really sorry. I know it can't be easy. Especially at this time of the year," Carter offered.

"It will get better, man," his brother Brad also added over the speaker phone.

"Will it?"

"It sure will. Give it time. You've been through a lot. Nothing can replace your family, but with time, you can move forward you know. Look at Evan."

"True. But he found someone."

"And he forgave himself for not being there when...well, you know."

"I know." Cameron's voice was soft and low. He didn't need them to continue on. He knew how heartbroken and crushed his brother Evan had been when his wife died while on a mountain climb. A climb that they were supposed to do together with their group. But it never happened. And like Cameron, he wasn't there for his loved one, when they were in grave danger.

He appreciated what his brothers were trying to do for him, by encouraging him. He really did. But this was something that was going to take time with him. He knew that. He could not skip any of the steps of grieving. But the trouble was, he felt stuck on one step. Denial.

"Well, you know I've got to take this long drive."

"Don't tell me you're out on the country road again."

"Just want to clear my mind. Going back to my cabin's just going to give me too much time to think."

"Maybe thinking is good. Sometimes," Brad offered.

"I don't know about now," Carter interjected. "Have you spoken to Pastor Johnson?" Carter asked.

Pastor Johnson had been in the family for three generations of the Charming family now. He was family. And he'd also married Carter to his sweetheart Paige, not too long ago.

"No, I haven't," Cameron replied.

"What's stopping you?"

"Time," he said.

"You've got plenty of it over the holidays, bro."

"Too much time," Cameron grumbled.

"Speaking of which, we need to kick your you know what during the snowball fight."

He grinned. Yes, last year he'd whooped their behind during a snowball charity fundraiser. It was a fun way to raise funds for the Children's new play center and a fun way to get wet in the snow while doing it too. The children had a blast watching the adults make a fool of themselves. And the kids each had their own snowball fun later amongst themselves too. He felt good helping out. But again, the loneliness swept over him like an avalanche once he returned home to his cabin. A place he spent less and less time each year after his family went to be with the Lord.

"It's on, bro," he said, before ending the call.

He continued to drive then he paused for a moment. He reached down to turn on the satellite radio, but the station would be playing Christmas tunes. The stations played all the Christmas songs both new and old, twenty-four hours a day during the month of December. His late wife had always tuned into that channel.

Should he play the songs now?

Would it dampen his mood?

Or would it make him feel closer to her?

He took a chance on the lonely quiet road and reached down to turn on the radio.

"All right, sweetheart. You always said we should play Christmas songs during the month of December," he spoke out loud as if speaking to his late wife. "Well, this one's for you." His voice was a whisper.

The song that came on after the DJ finished talking was *Do You Hear What I Hear?*

Sweet tune.

He and his late wife used to love singing that holiday song together. It was as if they were meant to sing it. It brought back memories that made him feel warm inside.

Just then, after fiddling with the radio station again to get it tuned again, his truck swerved slightly to the right.

Oh, no.

Chapter 5

Cat's eyes were fixed on the back of the cabin.

There was no back door.

How could that be?

It was then she remembered that this was not the original cabin she had selected. She'd changed her mind at the last moment and asked her agent to get a smaller cabin. She'd only seen the pictures over the Internet. She'd never seen it up close until now.

Great.

She heaved a sigh and rubbed her shoulders again trying to keep warm even though she was wearing her winter jacket.

Just then, she thought about her dear grandfather. She hoped he was warm and safe. A lot warmer than she was.

He deserved the best. She remembered when she had seen him at his home in New York, alone not long after Grandma had died. He was having a rough time then. There was no heat in that old house. Eventually, when the lease was up and he expressed he wanted to stay in a nice place with a lot of people just like him, she went with him to tour a few lovely retirement centers. He had worried about the price but she explained to him that she was doing well with her blog and social media page and that she was getting a nice large advance for her new book based on her blog. She assured him that she could take care of anything he needed.

And she meant it. The look on his face at the time melted her heart into a warm place.

She loved him and would do anything for him.

Speaking of which. That's why she had to get this book done this week to send to her agent. The publisher was waiting for her draft. That's what's paying the bills. If she couldn't hand in her draft and get over this block she'd been having in her creativity, she didn't know what would happen to her grandfather—or to her. She had to get this done. She'd already used some of the advance to pay the rent for this small cabin that wouldn't let her inside for some reason.

She held onto the side of the cottage as she carefully walked down the icy snowy side trying hard not to fall.

She had a funny leg as she liked to call it. It acted up sometimes. They did x-rays and ultrasounds and all kinds of tests and couldn't find anything wrong. Doc just told her to be careful. Sometimes the body acted up for no reason.

Well, she hoped it wouldn't do so now.

As she pressed her boot into the snow, hoping to have some sort of grip, she felt the ice move beneath her.

Oh, no. No, no, no, no, no.

She overstretched the muscle on the back of her lower leg, and...

Kaboom!

She slipped and tumbled down the sloping side of the cabin.

Oh, no. Please don't act up again, she pleaded with her left leg. *Please don't let me down now.*

Too late.

She went down like a sack of hay.

Her funny leg let her down, yet again. And on a night like this where she was all alone. Outside. Just her and the elements near a secluded cabin—just as she'd asked for. The saying flew into her mind.

Be careful what you ask for because you just might get it.

Intense pain swept through her body. A heavy ache twisted through her.

She fell and hurt herself on the ice.

She started to fade out.

The snowy night began to fade into a darkness.

Her eyelids became heavy...

Chapter 6

Cameron's detour ended up turning onto another side street. He was about to turn his truck around but for some reason he decided to drive further down the road, looking at the nice Christmas lights on some of the cabins.

All of the cabins had pretty decorations on them. Well, most of them. It was like a winter wonderland.

As he continued to drive down the street he noticed something in the distance. An isolated cabin. Cameron squinted as he slowed down his truck and looked through his windshield. He thought he saw something under the streetlight outside a cabin on the right. But he must be imagining it.

There was something on the front lawn.

Just then it moved.

Aw, man. That's a person.

He wondered what that fella was doing out on the ground in the middle of a snowstorm and on a cold night like tonight. Was the person drunk or something?

Maybe the Lord brought Cameron down this road for a reason.

He slowed down his truck and stopped the engine. He then pulled his coat on and adjusted his cowboy hat. He got out of the truck and slammed the door shut.

"Excuse me," he called out. "Need some help?"

He was taught in one of his emergency preparedness workshops to always ask if a person needed help. Never assume unless it's obvious or they could not speak for themselves.

He'd once thought a guy was attacking a woman in a park and went over there and grabbed the guy by his collar. Big mistake. The couple were newlywed and playing some sort of game, having fun. It didn't seem like it at the time. But he'd learned his lesson. Still, it looked obvious this fella on the ground needed help. He was practically down in the snow. And it didn't look as if he was making a snow angel either.

"I can't get up," the voice sounded. But it wasn't a man's voice. It was a beautiful soft voice of a woman.

"Ma'am, I'm right here," he said, moving closer to her. It was then that he saw her wavy shiny hair tucked under her hood. She was on her side. She turned her head to face him.

Her lovely eyes stared into his and his heart turned over in his chest.

"Are you hurt?" he asked, reaching for her.

"My leg. It just cramped up." She managed to turn over and reached for him and hugged her arms around his neck as he pulled her up.

He carefully assessed her movements to make sure she could get up safely. The sweet scent of her perfume wafted to his nose as the breeze blew around them. She smelled like an angel. Her fragrance was intoxicating and pleasing to his senses. He shifted his thoughts again. Why was he thinking of Ms. Beauty and her scent at a time like this? What was with this cowboy?

"Are you sure it's not broken? Did you fall?"

"No. I didn't fall that hard. I just slipped on the side slope there. The back of my leg hurts."

"You might've pulled your hamstring, Ma'am," he said. "Just let me carry you. You'll be all right. We need to get you inside."

She hopped as she walked with him. He was leading her to the cabin.

"Is this your place?"

"Yes."

"Good. Let's get you inside."

She stopped walking and she sighed deeply. She stared wordlessly at the cabin.

"You okay?" he asked gently, following her gaze.

Her eyes were so pretty. Long thick lashes framed her beautiful eyes. Her lips were shapely and red like strawberries. Her cheekbones high and defined. She was breathtaking.

Just then a recognition struck him.

"Cat?" he asked.

She looked into his eyes and the look of surprise filled her pretty face.

"Cameron?" she said.

It had been years since he'd seen her. Not since high school.

"Well look at that," he said. "Fancy seeing you again."

Relief washed over her. "I am so glad it's someone I know. I was worried about being found by a stranger." She chuckled.

He grinned. Just then something filled him inside. A warm feeling.

He remembered Cat from high school. They'd even dated once but then her folks died in some freak accident. It was horrible. He remembered how brave she was. He'd reached out to her then but at the time he was only a high school student and didn't know too much about emotional support. Her grandparents took her in and she'd moved to New York with them where they'd moved from Mistletoe.

Gosh, he'd missed her then.

But then he got on with his life and they never did keep in touch. He'd married, of course. And the last he'd heard was that she'd found someone in New York.

"Yes, what a surprise. Thank you for saving me out there. Never knew I'd see you again. Of course, we are in a small town but I was supposed to be spending time in this cabin for the month."

"Really?"

"Yes, I'm working on a book. I have a contract."

"A book? Congratulations!" He was always so proud of her. From the time he'd known her she'd always had her nose in a book. He'd admired her intellect back when they were in high school. He still couldn't get over seeing her again.

"Thanks."

"Well, you'd better get inside where it's warmer than out here," he said.

"I can't go inside," she told him.

"Why not?"

"The door won't let me."

He was confused about what she was talking about.

"The door won't *let* you?"

"Wrong key," she finally said. She reached into her purse and took out a bronze key.

"How did that happen?" he asked.

"My agent arranged for me to rent this cabin for a short time. He also got creative and gave me the wrong key. I guess he wanted to test my survival skills." She shook her head and grinned.

He liked her sense of humor. But this wasn't funny one bit. What kind of an agent would give a lady the wrong key to the door of her rented home?

"Okay. Well, right now, we have to get you out of the cold. You'll need to have a doctor look at that leg of yours to be sure you're okay."

"I know what it is."

"You do?"

"Yes," she said. "It happens once in a while."

"Talk about timing," he said.

"I know, right?"

He felt comfortable around her and could tell the feeling was mutual. It was as if time hadn't passed between them.

Just then she gave him a look of concern. Or was that sympathy?

"Something wrong?" he asked.

"Oh, no. It's been a while since I've been here. I read about your family. Oh gosh, Cameron, I am so sorry about your wife and stepdaughter. I'd sent some flowers when I heard."

His heart twisted in his chest.

He could only imagine what she must be thinking. She'd lost her own parents in a freak accident too.

Guilt and pain swept through his body leaving him numb and broken about his now late wife and stepdaughter—once again. He wished he'd been there to save them.

"Thank you." His voice was soft. He hoped she didn't hear the pain in his tone and the sorrow that he was feeling once again now. "I'm thankful to have my family help me get through this. Not just my church family but my extended family."

"Of course. During a time like that it's hard to get through grief without the support of family, friends and the church."

His family was well known in the town of Mistletoe. They owned the largest ranch in the district and had many community events going on. The Charming Ranch had been in the family since the late 1800s. Their great-grandfather was one of the earlier settlers when the town was new.

"So, you write a blog?" he asked, trying to change the subject. He didn't want to go down that painful road again right now.

"Yes. I write a woman's blog," she said, proudly. "I also get into some news stuff once in a while."

Interest in her blog piqued him. He'd always admired writers and authors. Being able to create stories to entertain and enlighten people was a spectacular gift. Writers shared stories that helped make sense of human behavior, about living and having dreams and about love.

His late wife had always loved reading blogs and listening to podcasts. She loved learning about people, learning about life. He missed her like crazy.

"I was wondering if I could ask you a favor," she said.

"What is it?" He wanted to help her. It was as if he wanted to do for her what he did not, could not do for his wife.

Was that why his path was directed down this road tonight? He had no idea why he continued to drive down this lonely path. Did the man upstairs have something to do with it? To help him re-write history somehow. To give him another chance?

No. It couldn't be. It just had to be a coincidence, right?

"I need you to force the door open or...see if you can get the window open," she said, regretfully.

He stopped for a minute. "You want me to break in and enter?"

"Yes. I mean no, of course not. I'm on the lease for the month." She looked apologetically. "I already paid up for the month."

He grinned and arched a brow. "Now how do I know you're telling me the truth?"

Chapter 7

"You're right. What was I thinking asking you that?" Cat placed her hands on her hips and sighed. "I could be pulling the wool over your eyes."

He sighed. "From the moment I met you in high school, you've always been an honest girl. Always doing the right thing. I don't doubt you for a minute," he said. "But there must be another way in."

"Really?" she asked as the cold winter wind blew around them.

He stood there looking deep into her eyes and her tummy did the butterflies thing.

Oh, my goodness.

He was more gorgeous than she'd remembered. Beautiful eyes and cheekbones that looked like they could dodge ice pellets.

And he had something her recent ex never had.

Integrity.

A warm feeling swept through her belly over Cameron, the tall, dark and handsome cowboy before her. And his cologne. What was that earthy beautiful scent? It was scrumptious.

Man, this cowboy was a true hero. An honest one too. A noble spirit. The do-the-right-thing type of cowboy. He not only stopped and turned around to help her before he knew who she was. But he had scruples too.

Cameron never changed being the sweet guy he'd always been.

Stop that, Cat.

You've sworn off dating, remember? You cannot get attracted to this cowboy in shining armour. Focus. Focus on your goals. You don't need any more handsome distractions after your ex.

She fought to sweep away her feelings of attraction to this cowboy, the guy she'd fallen in love with in high school. Of course, they'd grown apart. After her parents passed away and she moved to New York with her grandparents, they never did keep in touch. He'd also left town. This was way before texting and social media were popular. And by the time she'd moved to New York, it was too painful to keep in touch with anyone from Mistletoe at the time. It only brought back sad memories of losing her parents there.

"I know," she said feeling hopeless. "There must be another way in."

That was Cameron for you. Always the optimist. But she didn't feel too optimistic right now. Right now, she felt the bone chill of the wind on this wintery night.

If she could use her cell phone, she could have called her agent. She'd programmed his phone number into her phone and always used speed dial so she didn't have it by memory.

She had to admit it, as desperate as she felt right now to get inside to her warm cabin out from the cold windy winter night, she liked Cameron's stance. Find another way.

She was just so desperate that she hadn't realized that she couldn't ask someone to break into a cabin she was renting. What was she thinking?

Oh, right. Her brain was frozen right now.

That's it. She had brain freeze. Or common sense freeze.

The temperature seemed to plummet with each minute outside. She hugged herself to keep warm, rubbing her arms, wishing she'd worn her thicker Parka jacket.

"You want to sit in my truck and keep warm?"

"Nah, I'm good, thanks. Let's just figure out how to get inside."

He glanced at the large suitcase near the front door.

"So you moved back to work on your book."

"Yes. Just for the month. I'm so thankful to have this contract. I share my apartment in New York with some roommates. I needed a quiet space so I thought I'd move back and work on the book."

"That's smart of you. You were always so dedicated to whatever you set your heart on."

The words of encouragement brought a slither of joy to her heart. Her ex, her recent ex never said anything kind or sweet like that to her. What had she missed out on all these years?

Still, a gnawing feeling grabbed her.

Stay away from this sweet cowboy, Cat. You have no room in your life for relationships. Not anymore. Look at what happened with your recent ex.

She had to focus and not get too caught up on the holiday mood or feelings for Cameron. He was her past.

Besides, she just didn't seem to have much luck with men. After her recent ex broke her heart, she'd been so down for days, she didn't think she could get out of that funk and write again. There was no way she was going to take a chance on anything messing with her head—again.

"Thank you. I need to make sure the draft is ready by Christmas. It's what's paying my bills and taking care of my grandfather."

"That's so nice of you. How is he doing?"

"Thanks for asking. He's doing well." She blew out a puff of air.

"Listen, why don't you call your agent and let him know what's going on. Maybe he could get you the key."

"Good idea except I don't have any juice left on my phone and his number's programmed on it. I don't know it by heart—unfortunately."

"Oh, right. That sucks. Sorry to hear that."

"No worries, it's not your fault my battery's dead and I didn't memorize his number. Hey, you have your phone with you right?"

Silly question. Everyone had their phone with them. It was a part of who they were nowadays. But the question was, did he have enough battery power left on his phone to make a call?

Just then his phone rang, a melody sounded over the speaker. It was Away in a Manger.

She arched her brow. Interesting ring tone. She'd never heard anyone have that as a ring tone before. Cameron was a one of a kind sentimental cowboy.

"What's wrong?" he asked, answering his phone and telling the person he'd be with them soon.

"Oh, nothing. Did you change your ring tone to a Christmas song?" she asked. "Please tell me you don't have that song playing all year round?"

"Nope. Just for Christmas. I take it you're not into the Christmas spirit?"

She looked around. "Definitely not this year."

He took his call after excusing himself as they stood on her porch waiting for goodness knew what.

When he was finished, he turned to her.

"I've got some bad news."

"Oh, no. What's wrong?"

The last thing she needed now was bad news. What could be worse than what's happening now?

Chapter 8

Cameron was mesmerized by Cat's beauty, but he tried to stay focused. He liked her spunk and her energy but she was only here for the month and besides, he wasn't interested in pursuing anything.

He thought about the upcoming Barn Hall Dance. His folks had been onto him to bring a date but there was no way he would ask Cat. Besides, she was busy and he didn't want to date again.

"There's a weather warning in town," he continued. "Mayor's advising everyone to stay indoors."

"Oh, no."

"Yeah, I know the irony, right? But my brother works down at the town hall. He's heading home now. You'd better let me get you somewhere warm."

"I need to stay here. I don't have any family here. Not anymore."

"I see," he said. "Well you can always stay at my family ranch. You know that won't be any trouble. They'd love to see you again."

"That's very kind of you to offer, Cameron but I don't want to put you all out. I mean, it's not like we've been in touch all these years."

"Hey, you know it's no trouble. Our families go way back."

She smiled. Her smile was the prettiest he'd seen in a long time. There was something captivating about Cat. Something about her that resonated with him. Something familiar.

He just felt comfortable around her but he had to ignore those feelings. He was doing what any cowboy would do. He was helping this nice lady out—his high school friend whom he'd shared a date with once while they were students. He had to keep things in perspective.

They both knew that in a small town people knew each other and each other's business and nobody wanted to be the talk of the town. Not that he cared much if people thought he was seeing his high school friend or ex-girlfriend.

Mistletoe was also known for its breathtaking Christmas decorations and festive events at this time of the year, as well as its heavy snowstorms and blizzards. Still, he wanted to make sure she was safe.

"I just want to make sure you're going to be all right. You know my family's ranch. There are plenty of rooms in the main house. My mother would be happy to have you as a guest."

"Thank you. I'd love to," she said, looking around frantically. "But I really want to be here. I must get into my cabin tonight."

He adjusted his cowboy hat.

"Tell you what. Why don't we have a look around," he said as the heavy winds howled around them.

"What do you mean?"

"I mean," he said, looking around the outside of the cabin. "I'm sure the agent didn't just leave you high and dry."

He leaned down beside a rock. He grinned.

"What do you see?" she asked.

"You wouldn't believe it."

Chapter 9

"It's an envelope. That's what you found?" Cat asked incredulously. "My agent left me a letter under a *rock*?" She threw up her hands in disbelief. "What if someone else found it?"

Cat gently took the note that Cameron handed to her.

"Well, the good news is that it was well hidden," Cameron said. "And in this storm, I doubt anyone would even come around here looking for anything."

"True."

"And look on the bright side," he added. "At least it was under a rock, so the wind couldn't blow it away."

She glanced up at the tall, handsome cowboy. She'd almost forgotten how gorgeous he was. He always had the dreamiest set of eyes she'd ever seen on a man. And he had an air of optimism around him. Gorgeous inside and outside. Why didn't they ever get together or made it a point to stay in touch all these years?

He's the one that got away.

She couldn't help but notice his broad shoulders and tall physique. He must be around six feet four inches. A whole foot taller than she stood.

She felt the envelope and noticed there was something inside it.

She tore it open and found a note with a key attached.

She grinned and shook her head in disbelief.

That's Tom for you.

Tom was her agent and her old school friend. He was a part time agent and didn't have any other clients. He just had a love for literature and a few connections in the publishing world. He was an eccentric guy who sometimes did things in an unconventional way. He was also a part time real estate agent. He'd told her that hustling was the name of the game.

She read the note and chuckled.

"Everything okay?" he asked.

"I guess it should be now," she said. "Tom, my agent, left me this note saying he was sorry he sent me the wrong key. He also sold a cottage around here. He sells homes on the side. I guess he sold this cabin too as an investment for someone who wanted to rent it out. So I guess, I have the other customer's key and she or he has mine."

"He sells homes *and* manuscripts. Interesting," he said. "You might want to get the lock changed then," Cameron offered.

"Good thinking. I'll ask him if the new owners don't mind seeing as someone else could have the key to their cabin."

She tried the lock with the key from the envelope and nothing happened at first.

"You might want to give it a good wiggle, sometimes new locks take a little time to get in smoothly," Cameron said.

"I just hope he cut the right key this time," she said, hopefully.

She tried again and sure enough, it worked!

A wave of relief washed over Cat.

"Yay! We're in." She held out her hands as if welcoming her new home for the month.

"You mean you're in." He grinned.

"Well, you know what? We're a team now, aren't we?"

"I'll help you inside," he said, "Hold on to my shoulder."

Cameron grabbed her luggage with one hand and then held her carefully with his other free hand.

Her luggage was heavy—at least to her. It seemed like Cameron had no trouble holding it, like he was holding a feather pillow.

"Thank you," she said and held on to his firm shoulder. The cowboy looked as if he bench-pressed two hundred pounds of weight every day. He was fit as a horse.

He helped her into the foyer of her cozy new cabin as she hobbled on one foot.

"How's the pain, Cat?" he asked.

"Still there but it's getting better, thank the Lord. I just need to sit down."

"Sure, let me help you." He helped her to the couch where she sat down.

"Thank you so much," she said.

"Hey, no worries."

He then glanced around the cabin. "Nice cabin. I see its fully furnished."

"Yes, that was the deal. My agent said he'd have everything ready with new furniture fit for a writer in residence, so to speak. And he was right."

She looked around, pleased. There was a fireplace, a lovely rug in the center of the cabin's living room, a comfy chair and a couch with three square pillows, just in case she wanted to lie down and write. The hardwood floors shined like marble. The open-concept kitchen area had new cabinets. And the large windows gave her a nice view of the outside.

"Your agent sure did a good job."

"He did. I must remember to thank him later. And forgive him. Or maybe he should forgive *me*."

"For what?"

"For all those awful things I was thinking about him when I was locked outside of the cabin." She chuckled, shaking her head.

Cameron grinned.

"How could I ever thank you?" she asked her former high school friend, the cowboy who rescued her tonight.

"It's no problem. Really," he said.

She paused for a moment to ponder.

"Something on your mind?" he asked, gently.

"Yes. How did you find me?" she asked curiously.

He adjusted his cowboy hat. She loved when he did that. There was just something about a man in a cowboy hat, wearing a thick jacket, leather boots and jeans that mesmerized her.

He sighed.

"You wouldn't believe it," he said.

"Oh? Try me."

He grinned. "I'll tell you in a moment after we get you settled in here."

"Okay. You promise you won't forget."

"When it comes to you, Cat. I wouldn't forget anything."

She then glanced into Cameron's beautiful eyes then looked away as her heart fluttered in her chest.

She hoped he wouldn't see the rouge on her cheeks. She could tell she was blushing. Heat climbed to her cheeks. How could she still have feelings for Cameron? He was her past. She wasn't doing this.

"You know, I was thinking about your ring tone," she said, trying to change the subject as fast as she could.

"What about it?" he asked.

"Do you remember when we were in the Nativity Play at Christmas in grade nine?"

He smiled. And that cute dimple appeared on his cheeks just as it did in high school. She was always mesmerized by his charming smile but she tried not to glance at it now. Why did she bring up that Christmas play?

"You played Mary and I played Joseph," he said.

"Yes, I'll never forget that. I fumbled for my lines. I was so nervous."

"You were just perfect," he said.

He was very kind, she thought. She thought they always got along well together. Did she think he was too nice for her—just friend material back then. Well, she certainly didn't think so now but she was determined to brush that feeling aside. The feeling of comfort and familiarity with a nice old friend from her past. A guy in high school she'd once dated. A nice guy who was always so serious and focused on helping out on his family's ranch and looking after his younger siblings. He was everything her recent ex was not.

"I think we should take a look at your leg," he said, changing the subject.

Was there an awkward pause between them just now? Was that why he rushed to change the subject? It was for the best anyway. She didn't know why her mind went down memory lane just now. Her leg was the part of her that needed attention.

"Where does it hurt?" he asked her. "Can I touch here?"

"Sure" she said, swallowing hard.

"Does it hurt when I press there?"

The touch of his soft skin on hers, made her heart jump all over the place and butterflies in her tummy exploded.

No, this is wrong. I no longer have feelings for Cameron. He's my friend from my high school days. Nothing more.

Was she trying hard to convince herself?

"Uh, no. Yes. I mean, no."

"You sure?"

"Try there." She pointed to the spot behind her leg as she rested her foot on the empty stone coffee table in front of the couch.

He touched that to see if it hurt and she said just a little.

"Well," he said, after examining her leg. "You'll need to apply RICE."

"Rice?" she asked, perplexed.

"You know," he said, 'the acronym for rice: rest the injured muscle, ice the injured part to reduce any kind of swelling, compress the area, elevate the injured leg."

"Oh, right. RICE," she said, remembering her First Aid course she took years ago. "Of course."

Like seriously. How would she remember that acronym if she never had to use it. Okay, well, he was right about that.

"You can also take an Advil if that will help."

"You know what," she said. "It will subside. Actually, it's getting better."

He smiled. "You sure about that?"

He had no idea. But his presence was oddly comforting and relaxing—just as it had been in the past. She liked his aura and everything about his calm yet take-charge demeanor.

After he made sure her leg was stable on the table, he asked her if he could make her something to drink.

"That would be nice. I'm not sure if Tom stocked the fridge."

"I'll go see."

"Thank you." She touched his hand when he got up, not meaning to. The delightful feeling sent shivers dancing down her back.

Why was she reacting to this handsome cowboy like that?

She had to keep her mind focused on her work. There was no time for relationships. No time for dating. Not for the foreseeable future.

Still, she was grateful the good Lord sent an angel in disguise in her path when she was down on her face, *literally*, in the snow.

She was glad it was a good Samaritan, a church-going cowboy who spotted her first in the dark. Her beloved friend from high school. She was glad he spotted her when he did while driving down that lonely road at that time of night.

When he got back from the kitchen, he brought her a cup of steaming hot chocolate.

"Looks like Tom had you all stocked up nicely for your writing marathon."

She smiled appreciatively. "Thank you. And thank you for everything again. I don't want you to be waiting on me hand and foot. I'm sure you have places to go."

"I do, but I want to make sure you're all right first. You can barely weight bear on your one leg."

"I know," she agreed, reluctantly. "Why don't you make yourself some hot chocolate? Or would you prefer coffee?"

"I'm good, thanks," he said. "Just want to make sure you're okay."

He got up.

"What are you looking for?" she asked.

"A phone, a charger, an outlet. You need to have things close by to you so you won't have to get up all the time."

He began to arrange some of the furniture within safe and close distance to her.

"Do you need to lie down? What if you need to go to bed after I leave?"

"I'm sure the bedroom isn't far from here. I think it's just down the hall from what I remember from seeing the layout."

"Do you want me to take you there now?' he asked.

"Actually, the couch is really cozy," she said leaning into it. Just then her leg ached mercilessly again. A sharp pain then shot through her leg at the back.

Cameron was right. She wouldn't do too well on her own right now. What if she fell if she tried to get up?

What would she do then?

He placed her phone charger next to her and began to charge her phone.

Man, he was so considerate. Her recent ex was nothing like Cameron. Once, when she'd sprained her wrist, he didn't even show any sense of concern, not like Cameron.

"You want me to start the fire in the fireplace?" he asked, helpfully.

"Actually, that would be nice. But do you have all the things you need?"

He grinned. "There's wood by the side there. Looks like Tom had you all set up."

She smiled. "Sorry, I might be from the small town but I identify as a city girl. And I wouldn't know a fireplace starter if I saw one."

"It's all right. Glad to help."

He paused for a moment. I'm going to show you how to set this up, and what to do when the wood is finished burning."

"Sounds like a plan," she said.

"Just wait here a minute," he said, softly.

"Why? Where are you going?"

"Just making sure the chimney's open."

After everything was set up, Cameron made sure safety was in place.

"You are a true hero," she said. "I can't thank you enough."

She realized she sounded like a broken record repeating herself over and over. She just hadn't been around a man like that who was so helpful. Her recent ex certainly wasn't. She just wanted Cameron to know that she really appreciated what he was doing for her. What would she have done all alone out there injured in the snow on a cold night like tonight?

"You know something," she said. "It was really good of you to stop and reach out to me while I was lying flat on the snow."

"Aww, it's nothing. Any man would have done the same."

"No, I'm afraid not."

"What do you mean?" he asked, genuinely puzzled.

"My ex, the guy I was dating in New York, wouldn't have stopped. We were walking in the town once and there was a guy who looked homeless lying down flat on his face."

"Oh, no. Did you check to see if he was all right?" Cameron asked, concerned.

"Well, I did. I told my ex, whom I will not mention his name," she said, shaking her head. "I told him we should go and see if the man's all right."

"And? What did he say?"

"I won't use his words but he wasn't very kind about it and said he was probably intoxicated to put it lightly. I tried to call out to the man to see if he was all right. He looked as if he was having some sort of crisis. At the end of the day, he's a human being. And no one knows why a person ends up in the place they do," she said.

"Good on you," Cameron said.

She really felt Cameron's warm sentiment. This cowboy was all heart.

"So I took out my cell phone while my ex walked on, and I called the emergency."

"Atta girl."

"Thanks. It turned out that the man had a stroke and paramedics got there in time. I just shiver to think of what would've happened if no one had stopped. I should have seen my ex was no good at the time. We didn't last much longer after that. Don't get me wrong, it wasn't just that incident, it was other things I'd noticed. He'd just finished college and was on his way with his career and..." She stopped.

She could tell Cameron wanted to hear more. She didn't want to tell him that she'd caught her ex cheating on her with some dancer—a former college classmate in the Dancing Arts program.

"I'm sorry, I don't mean to babble on."

"You're not babbling, Cat. It's okay to get things off your chest."

Validation. He was validating me. He has no idea what that means to me. But I will not get too caught up in that. He's a good friend. An old friend from high school. Someone I appreciate and I don't want to get ahead of myself or risk messing things up between us.

"Thank you," she said, appreciatively. "What would I have done without you, tonight?"

He grinned. "Just get well and share your book with the world," he said.

Man, Cameron was so nice. It was refreshing to be around a guy like that.

Her phone pinged. The battery was slowly charging it. It had some power in it now. At least 1% and counting.

"I really appreciate you doing that for me. Can't believe my phone was completely dead."

"It'll be fine soon. Shouldn't take too long to charge. It's happened to me before too while on the road all day."

"I find that hard to believe," she said. "You seem so organized."

He grinned and his boyish grin produced a cute dimple on his cheek. He was adorable. Charming. In other words, he lived up to his last name. She knew the Charming brothers and their small-town charm. They were strong cowboys with a heart of gold.

"Actually, you'd be surprised when you're busy running errands all day," he said.

"Speaking of which, were you running errands when you drove down this road?" she asked him.

"Actually no. You'd be surprised. Coming down this road wasn't planned." He then grinned and looked up towards the ceiling of the cabin for a split second. "Well, at least not by me."

She smiled and agreed. "I think someone's looking out for me."

"You better believe that. I was driving and intended to turn one direction but my truck took me down here. And when I tried to turn around something told me not to."

"It was meant to be," she said.

"Looks like the man upstairs wanted us to cross paths this evening."

"Yes, it sure looks like it," she said. "You know I'm going to church on Christmas morning. I haven't been in months but I will this year."

"In months? How come?"

"I don't celebrate Christmas. Not anymore. My grandfather is my only surviving close relative now and he doesn't either."

"I'm sorry to hear that."

"It's okay. Anyway, we vowed to never get hung up on the holiday celebrations again after Grandma passed."

"I can see it must be difficult for you. But you something, I think you'd feel different with the Christmas spirit if you give it another chance.."

"You think so?"

"Yes."

"Do you still celebrate it...?"

He looked down for a moment. "Yes, I do now. I have to."

"You *have* to?" She arched a brow.

"Yes. My wife and stepdaughter used to celebrate it with me. And after they passed," he said, emotion in his voice.

He stared into the fireplace. The orange flames created a nice glow on his face.

Cat wanted to reach out and hug him. Her heart broke for what he'd been through. She could not imagine what it must be like. He'd lost so much, yet he had so much to be thankful for.

"I decided," he continued, "to carry on the things that made them happy when they were here. Actually, things that made us all happy. It's a way to not just bring the spirit of the holiday around but their memories as well."

"That's so noble of you," she said, softly.

"Just doing the right thing," he said.

"So were you celebrating tonight?" she asked, wanting to know more. She wanted to help him celebrate it. Even though she hadn't done so in many years.

"Well, I was at the children's center at the hospital volunteering and bringing Christmas gifts for the kids there."

"I think that's wonderful of you," she said.

"Hey, I've got some spare time now. Besides, we're always looking for volunteers. Not everyone has the time. We even have this center for creative expression for teens having trouble with expressing their feelings."

"Oh, my goodness. I would love to help out but I don't know if I'd have time," she said regretfully.

"Hey, no worries. Of course, you'll be working on your book."

"If I finish early, I'll let you know," she said, hopefully.

"That sounds good! That would be amazing if you could take part in the creative writing therapy workshops."

"I'm sure it would."

A feeling of dread swept over her. She was never going to see her old friend, this handsome and caring cowboy, again after tonight. They'd probably go their separate ways and lose touch again as they had in the past. She knew she was going to be busy focusing on her book and then, by Christmas, she'd be back in New York.

Just then, they were inches from each other and she thought he was about to kiss her. Was he going to kiss her?

A second later, he pulled away.

That had to be her imagination. Why would he want to kiss her when they'd only just become re-acquainted after all these years?

Silly girl.

How embarrassing.

"So how's your book coming along?" he asked, probably trying to change the mood.

"Well, it's practically finished. I just have to go through the draft and make sure to tweak it and add some editorial changes. The final draft is due very soon. I'm so thankful I can take care of Grandpa with the money from my work."

"You're a real trooper, you know that?" he said.

"I try. Family is everything," she added.

"I like the way you think." He looked as if he were deep in thought for a moment.

"Are you okay?" she asked, trying to pretend she didn't try to kiss him earlier.

"I'm good. You're right though. Family is everything."

She could kick herself.

He'd lost *his* family. Why, oh, why did she bring it up?

She hoped one day, he'd be able to move forward despite the pain of losing his wife and child and find some form of happiness later.

Cat thought about that for a moment. She had lost so much in her life as well. So many people in so many ways, but she always created a wall around her heart to distance herself.

Just then a thought struck her.

Could she ask this caring and charismatic cowboy one last favor?

Chapter 10

"Could I ask you another favor?" Cat asked, her pretty eyes wide and charming. "I know I don't deserve it."

"What makes you say that?"

She was humble as warm apple pie, yet so beautiful and acted as if she didn't know it. He was mesmerized by her beauty, her spirit, her aura. He'd never felt this way about any woman since his wife passed. He never thought he ever would again.

"I don't know," she said. "You've done more than enough for me."

"Try me."

"Would you like to help me decorate this cozy little cabin?" Cat said, with a cute innocent expression on her face.

"You're having a change of heart?"

"Well, I almost died out there in the snow if it weren't for the good Lord bringing you into my path. I think it would be nice to get back into putting up festive decorations to celebrate the true meaning of the season. It's the very least I could do."

He found her absolutely charming. Adorable.

And just a moment ago, he felt a pulse between them. Their faces, their lips were so close and he wanted to kiss her. But he couldn't. He wouldn't. It was just the passing moment. That's all it was. She was his former high school girlfriend, a good friend from the past. Nothing more.

He didn't want to think about getting involved with another woman. Not now. Maybe never.

Though, he had to admit, this was the first time he'd ever felt so close to a woman, since his wife went to be with the Lord.

This was the first time in a long while he'd felt so comfortable, so wanted, so secure for some reason.

Was the man upstairs trying to tell him something? Show him a sign?

He'd heard of instant attraction before. Kismet. He just didn't believe in it. And he'd dated Cat in high school but this was different. More intense. Still, he didn't want to get his hopes up.

If he thought about it, he had been devastated since his wife and child died, that he wasn't able to save them. So, now, even though this situation wasn't the same thing, not even close, he was able to save someone else from danger.

Was this the reason he was brought down this lonely road? He had to admit it was perfect timing. Cat could have frozen to death out there on the cold night if he hadn't gotten there in time. Her leg had seized up. That had happened to him once and it took him hours for his leg to feel all right to move.

What if she'd been there for hours in the frigid temperature?

He tried not to think about that but just thanked the Lord he was there in time.

She was special.

There was just something about her aura that connected to him in a beautiful way. He hoped to see her again before she went back to New York.

"So, you've got the Christmas spirit back, have you?" he asked with a grin.

"You'd better believe it, cowboy. How about it?"

Her smile was wide and beautiful.

"Sure, why not?"

Chapter 11

Cat

The following week, after Cat had time to settle into her cabin and get some writing done, she took a stroll through the Mistletoe Market with Cameron to hunt for some Christmas decorations. What was she doing? She shouldn't be having fun with her ex from high school. She should be getting ready to go back to New York. But she just couldn't help herself. It was just like the old days. Spending quality time with the one you feel good about.

Cameron had been so sweet to her over the past week, making sure she had enough wood for her fireplace and making sure her fridge and cupboards were stocked with enough food to last her for the duration of her stay.

"You really don't have to," she'd told him.

"Hey, it's no trouble," he'd said, casually.

For the first time she had a chance to be Cat. It was a change having someone look out for her instead of the other way around.

With her ex, she was always making sure he was okay and making sure he had his assignments done because she wanted to see him succeed. And for what? For him to turn around and break her heart?

She didn't want to fill her mind with her recent ex right now. She had to get rid of that habit.

Count your blessings, not your troubles.

That's what her grandfather always told her and she was going to practice doing that from now on. It was so easy to do whenever she was around Cameron. He had that special aura around him.

They picked up gold ornaments for her Christmas tree at her cabin and later went to the tree lot to pick out a small tree.

Later, Cameron had helped her set it all up. They had a ball of fun in each other's company. He had such a fine sense of humor. She regretted that she didn't work harder to keep in touch—before he got married, of course.

***

"Where's Cat?" the friendly voice on the other end of the phone asked with a chuckle later that afternoon. "What happened to her?"

"Grandpa, it's me," Cat answered, cheerfully.

"I know, darling. I was only pulling your leg. You just sound like a different person."

"I do?"

"You seem more relaxed. Cheerful. You sound like my granddaughter again. So, who is the lucky guy?"

She playfully rolled her eyes and grinned as she pressed the phone to her right ear.

"Very funny, Grandpa." She sat by the window with her laptop open and peered out at the lovely snow-covered lake behind her cabin.

The town was blanketed in a lovely coat of white. The pine trees capped with snow. Everything seemed so light for a change. She really liked the cozy atmosphere of Mistletoe. A huge change from her life in the city.

"What makes you think it's about a guy?" she asked him.

"Because you sound like you're in love."

A warm feeling slid over her at that thought followed by a wave of anxiety.

No, it couldn't be. She swore she would never enter into a relationship again. Not for now. She was going to focus on her career for a change. Focus on Cat.

Sure, she was having a wonderful time with Cameron in Mistletoe but he was her friend from high school, a cowboy from a small town and she was a city girl from the big city.

Her life was in New York now. The last time she'd dropped everything for a guy, it had backfired on her. Never again.

She sighed deeply. "I was locked out of my cabin and this really nice cowboy helped me out. We're just friends. Nothing more. Nothing will come of it, Grandpa."

"Locked out of your cabin?" her grandfather sounded alarmed.

"Oh, no, I'm fine. Thanks to Cameron. He spotted me in the snow and..." She bit down on her lower lip. She didn't want to tell him too much to get him worried. "I'm fine though. It all worked out. And Cameron and I got back to talking. You remember Cameron."

"Oh, right. The Charmings' boy. A fine young man he is. So sad about his late wife and stepdaughter."

"I know. A horrible tragedy."

"How is he coping?"

"He's doing as best as he could. I was so glad we met up again though."

"So am I. You two always did get along together. I remember you would write about him when you were in high school."

A grin curved her lips. She did write about him back then, didn't she?

"Oh, come on now," her grandfather said. "It's a sign."

"A sign?"

"Yes, it's a sign to move on. Maybe you two could..."

"Grandpa," she said lovingly, before he could get to finish. She didn't want to get her hopes up for nothing—or his. "It's not like that."

"How do you know? You know sometimes the good Lord directs our steps. We need to open our eyes and our hearts."

She swallowed hard. She knew her grandfather was right. But the trouble was, she was afraid. Afraid of getting hurt again.

***

Carter

A couple more weeks had passed by and Cameron and Cat ended up decorating her small cabin while she worked on her manuscript. She'd told him that she had writer's block until they met and now she felt at ease to write.

They even spent time at the Children's Hospital and Cat had given the teens some fun writing exercises to do. They loved her. And he could see the love on her face. She would be great with her own kids if she ever became a mother.

He had no idea why he thought that but he just did.

They went out to dinner at the Mistletoe Steak House and later spent time shopping for ornaments at the Christmas market. They even had a few fun snow fights and built a snowman together.

By the week before Christmas, Cat told him she had to go back to the New York to her apartment and hand in her manuscript.

She would be gone. Just like the feelings of joy he'd had over the past few weeks with her.

Her cabin was just a temporary setup. He'd hoped she would want to stay in Mistletoe, the town she grew up in, but he understood.

"So you're leaving for good?" he asked, as they rode horses at the Charming Ranch. He'd taken her on a trail ride and she loved the ranch.

"I have to. It's been great here, but...I don't belong in a small town. Not anymore"

"What makes you say that?"

"I'm a city girl at heart. Don't get me wrong, it's nice and quiet here, but..." She sighed as the horse continued to move on the trail.

"I was hoping you'd come to the Charming Ranch Barn Hall Christmas Dance."

"Oh, I've heard about that. The Annual Barn Hall Dance, right?"

"That's right?"

"I have a flight out tonight. I'm going to see Grandpa on Christmas Day and then...I guess work on my next book and my New Year's blog."

"Of course." He tried to hide his disappointment. But he admired her for her work.

"You brought the spirit of the holidays back and I'm so grateful for you. For that and for saving my life out there."

Saving her life.

He'd saved her life, hadn't he? Hearing her say it brought something inside his heart. It lightened the burden he'd been carrying—even if just a little. He guessed their paths were just meant to cross briefly before going back to their own lives. She received the spirit of the holidays and he received a way to forgive himself. A gift they could not deny was a miracle.

But sadly, it looked as if their moment was about to end. Would he ever see her again?

Chapter 12

"You look miserable today son," Cameron's mother said to him at the main house. "What happened? You were so happy these past few weeks."

"I know," he said, not realizing his tone was low until it was too late. "Cat's going back to New York."

"Oh, I'm so sorry to hear that."

"Yeah, she won't be able to make it to the barn hall dance."

"Now *that's* a shame. I was hoping you two would..."

He arched a brow. "Would do what, Ma?"

"Oh, nothing."

"Ma, what have you been up to?"

He folded his arms across his chest.

"Oh, nothing son. It's just that your brothers have gotten lucky under that old mistletoe in the barn. You know kissing under the mistletoe brings good luck to the couple under it."

He grinned and shook his head. I think that time has passed for me, Ma. I've had my chance with a family."

"Now, son. Don't give up on love. You know as I said to your brothers, the man upstairs will give you beauty for ashes. All you need to do is have a little faith and a little hope. Even faith as small as a mustard seed. Nothing can ever replace your beautiful family; may they rest in heavenly peace. But they would want you to be happy. There's such a thing as second chances."

Cameron would love to believe so. He could have tried harder to get Cat to stay but he didn't want to risk being hurt again. But maybe his mother was right. His brothers had taken a chance on finding love again and it worked out for them. The problem was, would it work out for Cameron too? Or was he destined to remain single for the rest of his life. Cat probably wanted to move on and find some city guy to spend the rest of her life with.

Her life was in New York now, not in the small town of Mistletoe. She said it herself; she might be from the small town but she identified as a city girl. Would she even be happy there with him? His life was the ranch, his family, the Mistletoe church and the children's center. He didn't have room in his life for anything else. Or anyone else. Or was it because he was afraid to make room for anyone else?

Chapter 13

The Annual Charming Ranch Christmas Barn Hall Dance was upon them.

It seemed as if everyone in the town of Mistletoe made it to the celebration. The barn hall was decorated in bright festive lights and garlands around. Music from the speakers played. Earlier that day, they spent the morning in Church after breakfast.

Luncheon was served at the homeless shelter in town. Then it was the dinner. And now the dance.

The Charming family liked to keep up the tradition that had been in the family for over a hundred years.

It was Christmas. And although he felt happy for the guests filing into the barn, there was something missing inside him.

There was something missing from his life.

Cat.

He'd only just became reacquainted with her this month, yet she made a deep impression on him. It was as if they'd always been together all these years without missing a beat. It was as if they'd never been apart.

The re-connection felt so real.

Was this really a second chance?

Well, if it was, it looked as if his second chance had flown back to New York.

They'd spent the last few weeks, sharing so much joy. Playing Mr. and Mrs. Santa Clause for the kids at the hospital. Sharing laughter and stories. How could he gave gotten it all wrong?

How could it have ended so soon?

Should he have asked her to stay?

But that wouldn't be fair to her, would it?

She had a life outside of him. And that life was calling to her. It wanted her back.

"You look gloomy, bro," his brother Carter said, as a lively version of O Holy Night played over the speakers. "Where's Cat?"

Cat had a chance to spend time with Cameron's family when she'd finished the draft of her book. They all loved her—as they always had. She really made an impression on them this month, especially his mother who told him it was so good to see him smile again.

"She's on a flight to New York," Cameron said, his heart aching at those words.

"New York?"

"Yes, she's turning in her manuscript and then working on her blog. She has a lot of sponsors she has to please."

"Looks like you're not one of them."

"Nope."

"Hey, man, I'm really sorry about that. You two looked so happy these past few weeks."

A knot tightened in his stomach. Yes, he had been happy, but just as with his late wife and child, it was as if happiness wasn't meant to last around him.

He tried to push the negative thought out of his head, his heart, but it wasn't easy.

Carter then turned back to Cameron and said, "Bro, how's your eyesight?"

His brother and he always played around and teased each other.

"It's fine, why?"

"Oh, nothing. It's just that you said Cat was on a flight to New York. You sure about that now?" Carter arched a brow.

When Cameron turned around, his heart leaped inside his chest.

"Cat?" he said as she walked into the Barn Hall.

She looked breathtaking.

She wore her hair down and had the most beautiful satin red festive dress that seemed to hug her curves. Her lipstick matched her dress, the rouge was like a delicious shade of strawberry.

Was this real?

Was he imagining this?

"Hey, cowboy," she said to him when they were inches apart.

"Hey, Cat. You look amazing! Beautiful."

Her cheeks colored.

"Thank you. So do you. I mean you look handsome."

"Thanks. I thought you were in New York?"

"I had a change of plans."

"You did."

"Well, I had a change of heart. I had so much fun here and I decided to extend my rent on the cabin. I want to stay here in Mistletoe."

"But what about your grandfather?"

"He asked me about my time here, and I told him. He told me he was having fun at the retirement center and told me he'd see me in the New Year. He insisted I stay here. He's still not into celebrating Christmas right now. But I have a feeling I'm going to change his mind soon."

A warm feeling came over Cameron.

"I think he'd be happy to see you happy."

She chuckled. "I was afraid," she said to him.

"Afraid of what?"

"Of taking a chance on being with someone again after you know who."

He grinned.

"And now?" he asked, reassuringly.

"And now, I'm thinking why would I paint my future with the colors of the past? The past is gone. You and I have known each other since high school. You're such a good guy, Cameron. I love the way I feel when I'm with you."

"I love the way I feel when I'm with you too. I know it's hard. Trust me. But as Ma says, sometimes we've just got to put our trust in doing the right thing. Knowing that He'll always look out for us."

"Amen to that."

"Would you like to dance?" he asked.

"I'd love to."

They moved onto the dance floor and danced, touching her skin while holding her hand gave him a light feeling.

After the dance, she looked up.

"Is that the famous mistletoe?" she asked.

"You've heard about it then," he said, unable to hide his grin.

"Everyone has. The legend is that whoever kisses under it will have good luck and a happy relationship."

"It actually worked out well for two of my brothers. You see them over there?" Cameron pointed out.

"Wow, you mean their wives met them here?"

"Well, sort of."

She leaned closer to him.

A smile curved the corners of his lips.

"Well, cowboy," she said. "How about it?"

He leaned closer to her and they kissed under the mistletoe, her lips were as soft as they looked. The kiss was magical. Delight shivered through him.

She's the one.

That thought just slid through him. He never thought he could be happy again but right now he wanted to make Cat as happy as he felt right now.

They sealed their future with the mistletoe kiss just as his brothers had done. And he looked forward to spending more time with Cat and a future filled with hope and happiness.

***

Thank you for reading *Cowboy for Christmas (Rescued by the Cowboy at Christmas Book 3)*. To be notified of future stories, you can send us an email at pageturningstories@gmail.com .